Please,
Mr. Crocodile!

For Min — T. S.
For Floyd, Stuart and Lorna — R. M.

Barefoot Poetry Collections
an imprint of
Barefoot Books
37 West 17th Street
4th Floor East
New York, New York
10010

Printed on 100% acid-free paper
Illustrations prepared in watercolor on Bockingford 200gsm watercolor paper.

Graphic design by Amesbury Grzelinski Ltd, England
Typeset in Bernhard Modern and Heatwave.
Color separation by Grafiscan, Italy
Printed and bound in Singapore by Tien Wah Press (Pte) Ltd

1 3 5 7 9 8 6 4 2

Publisher Cataloging-in-Publication Data

Please, Mr. Crocodile! : poems about animals /
complied by Tessa Strickland ; illustrated by Rosslyn
Moran.—1st ed.
[40]p. : col. ill. ;   cm.
Summary: An anthology of animal poems for young
readers. Contains verses by poets as diverse as William
Wordsworth, Ogden Nash and Rhoda Gersten,
accompanied by magical, bright and playful illustrations.
ISBN 1-902283-62-7
1.Animals -- Juvenile poetry. 2. Children's poetry. I. Strickland, Tessa.
II. Moran, Rosslyn, ill. III. Title.
808.819/ 362--dc21 1999 AC   CIP

Please,
Mr. Crocodile !

Poems About Animals

compiled by Tessa Strickland

illustrated by Rosslyn Moran

BAREFOOT BOOKS

Contents

Introduction

When I set out to compile *Please, Mr. Crocodile!* I had three aims. First, I wanted to offer children a collection that would provide a natural and enjoyable progression from the straightforward rhyme and repetition of nursery rhymes to the more complex, challenging and intriguing mysteries of poetry. Then, I was concerned to bring together as many different voices as possible, and pay tribute to some of the marvelous new talent that abounds in this genre, but is often underrepresented in anthologies. And finally, I wanted to celebrate the glorious diversity of the animal kingdom and share with my young audience the love of animals that has accompanied me through my life.

As a child growing up in the countryside of north England and surrounded by the creatures typical of that region, my ear was as much attuned to the sounds of the animal world as those of the human world. At the same time, I was fascinated by the sound patterns of the poems I learned by heart at school and it became apparent to me at an early stage how well the medium of poetry suits our human response to, and engagement with, the animal realm. So in making my selections for this anthology, I looked for as much variety as possible in effective use of language, and I sought out poems that in one way or another succeed in crystallizing a particular animal's character and/or the poet's feelings about that animal.

In some cases, the language of these poems is engagingly direct and straightforward, as in Joan Horton's description of a gray squirrel: "Find an acorn; crack it, crunch it/Nibble, nibble, munch, munch, munch it."

In others, it is rich in metaphor, as with Joseph Payne Brennan's owl who is "a drift of smoke...whispering wings/making the sound of silk unfurling." Several of the poems use the disciplines of meter and rhyme; but others are marvelous examples of how the best poetry is as much about alliteration and onomatopoeia as about formal rhyme schemes. A splendid example of this is Julie Holder's riotous "The Corn Scratch Kwa Kwa Hen."

Humor, fear and wonder are recurrent aspects of our response to animals. Countee Cullen exploits humor brilliantly with "First Came L. E. Phant's Letter" and so does Ogden Nash with his classic "An Introduction to Dogs," and Richard Edwards with "Our Pond." For a one-liner that sums up the shock of encountering a snake, it is hard to beat Emily Dickinson's "zero to the bone," while the profound quiet of the jungle at night is marvelously evoked by Joan Cass in "The Tiger": "Silently he moves/and gives/the soft sound of his padded feet/back to the silent night."

With creatures domestic and wild from many parts of the world, and with poets both new and well-known from both sides of the Atlantic, *Please, Mr. Crocodile!* is a collection for children and adults everywhere to laugh at, and to learn from. All poetry is meant to be read aloud, and above all, to be enjoyed. I hope that you will enjoy sharing the poems with the children in your lives, just for the delight of it as well as for the creatures of fin, fur and wing who inhabit these pages.

Tessa Strickland

Beasts and Birds

The dog will come when he is called,
    The cat will walk away;
The monkey's cheek is very bald,
    The goat is fond of play.
The parrot is a prate-apace,
    Yet knows not what she says;
The noble horse will win the race,
    Or draw you in a chaise.

The pig is not a feeder nice,
    The squirrel loves a nut,
The wolf would eat you in a trice,
    The buzzard's eyes are shut.
The lark sings high up in the air,
    The linnet in the tree;
The swan he has a bosom fair,
    And who so proud as he?

Adelaide O'Keeffe

Warm Paws

Snow
melts

Ice
thaws

Warm
paws

Brian Patten

10

Please, Mr. Crocodile!

Please, Mr. Crocodile,
May we cross the water,
To see your ugly daughter
Floating on the water
Like a cup and saucer?

Anon.

The Shark

A treacherous monster is the Shark,
He never makes the least remark.

And when he sees you on the sand,
He doesn't seem to want to land.

He watches you take off your clothes,
And not the least excitement shows.

His eyes do not grow bright or roll,
He has astounding self-control.

He waits till you are quite undressed,
And seems to take no interest.

And when towards the sea you leap,
He looks as if he were asleep.

But when you once get in his range,
His whole demeanor seems to change.

He throws his body right about,
And his true character comes out.

It's no use crying or appealing,
He seems to lose all decent feeling.

After this warning you will wish
To keep clear of this treacherous fish.

His back is black, his stomach white,
He has a very dangerous bite.

Lord Alfred Douglas

13

Ducks' Ditty

All along the backwater,
Through the rushes tall,
Ducks are a-dabbling,
Up tails all!

Ducks' tails, drakes' tails,
Yellow feet a-quiver,
Yellow bills all out of sight
Busy in the river!

Slushy green undergrowth
Where the roach swim —
Here we keep our larder,
Cool and full and dim.

Every one for what he likes!
We like to be
Heads down, tails up,
Dabbling free!

High in the blue above
Swifts whirl and call —
We are down a-dabbling
Up tails all!

Kenneth Grahame

14

An Introduction to Dogs

The dog is man's best friend.
He has a tail on one end.
Up in front he has teeth.
And four legs underneath.

Dogs like to bark.
They like it best after dark.
They not only frighten prowlers away
But also hold the sandman at bay.

A dog that is indoors
To be let out implores.
You let him out and what then?
He wants back in again.

Dogs display reluctance and wrath
If you try to give them a bath.
They bury bones in hideaways
And half the time they trot sideaways.

They cheer up people who are frowning,
And rescue people who are drowning,
They also track mud on beds,
And chew people's clothes to shreds.

Dogs in the country have fun.
They run and run and run.
But in the city this species
Is dragged around on leashes.

Dogs are upright as a steeple
And much more loyal than people.

Ogden Nash

17

First Came L. E. Phant's Letter

Dear Noah: Please save me a spot
Exposed to the sun, where the Mice are not;
But if I must share my chamber, the Ant
Is the one I should welcome. Yours: L. E. Phant

Countee Cullen

Lion

The name opens wide
as soon as you
speak it   L   I
O   N   Jaw unhinges
teeth flash white
sharp   against all that
red

From all the best possible
choices   FLEA   TOAD
PEACOCK   he picked this
for himself   LION
the only one he could say
while   ROARING!

Barbara Juster Esbensen

Nicholas Nye

Nicholas Nye was lean and gray,
    Lame of a leg and old,
More than a score of donkey's years
    He had seen since he was foaled;
He munched the thistles, purple and spiked,
    Would sometimes stop and sigh,
And turn his head, as if he said,
    "Poor Nicholas Nye!"

Alone with his shadow he'd drowse in the meadow,
    Lazily swinging his tail;
At break of day he used to bray, —
    Not much too hearty and hale.
But a wonderful gumption was under his skin,
    And a clear calm light in his eye,
And once in a while he would smile a smile
    Would Nicholas Nye.

Seem to be smiling at me, he would,
    From his bush, in the corner, of may —
Bony and ownerless, widowed and worn,
    Knobble-kneed, lonely and gray;
And over the grass would seem to pass
    'Neath the deep dark blue of the sky,
Something better than words between me
    And Nicholas Nye.

Walter de la Mare

20

The Corn Scratch Kwa Kwa Hen

And the Corn Scratch Kwa Kwa Hen
Heard the grumbling rumbling belly
Of the Slink Back Brush Tail Fox
A whole field away.

And she said to her sisters in the henhouse,
"Sisters, that Slink Back Brush Tail Fox
Will come and here's what we must do,"
And she whispered in their sharp sharp ears, "kwa kwa."

And when that Slink Back Brush Tail Fox
Came over the field at night,
She heard his paw slide on a leaf,
And the Corn Scratch Kwa Kwa Hen and her sisters
Opened their beaks and —

"KWA!"
The moon jumped
And the Chooky Chook Chicks
Hid under the straw and giggled,
It was the **LOUDEST KWA** in the world.

22

And the Log Dog and the Scat Cat
And the Brat Rat and the House Mouse
And the Don't Harm Her Farmer
And his Life Wife and their Shorter Daughter
And their One Son came running,

On their slip slop, flip flop,
Scatter clatter, slick flick, tickly feet
And they opened their mouths and shouted —

"FOX!"
And it was the **LOUDEST NAME** in the world.
And the Slink Back Brush Tail Fox
Ran over the fields and far away
And hid in a hole with his grumbling rumbling belly.

And the Corn Scratch Kwa Kwa Hen
Tucked the Chooky Chook Chicks under her feathers
And said "kwa,"
And it was the softest kwa in the world.

Julie Holder

23

Hyena

The scruffy one
who eats the meat
together with the bag
in which it is kept.
The greedy one
who eats the mother
and does not spare the child.
God's bandy-legged creature.
Killer in the night.

Yoruba, Nigeria
Translated by Ulli Beier

The Spider

I'm told that the spider
Has coiled up inside her
Enough silky material
To spin an aerial
One-way track
to the moon and back;
Whilst I
Cannot even catch a fly.

Frank Collymore

The Kitten Playing with the Falling Leaves

See the kitten on the wall
Sporting with the leaves that fall!
Withered leaves, one, two, and three,
From the lofty elder-tree.
Through the calm and frosty air
Of this morning bright and fair
Eddying round and round they sink
Softly, slowly. — One might think,
From the motions that are made,
Every little leaf conveyed
Some small fairy, hither tending,
To this lower world descending.
— But the kitten how she starts!
Crouches, stretches, paws, and darts:
First at one, and then its fellow,
Just as light, and just as yellow:
There are many now — now one —
Now they stop and there are none.
What intentness of desire
In her up-turned eye of fire!
With a tiger-leap half way,
Now she meets the coming prey.
Lets it go at last, and then
Has it in her power again.

William Wordsworth

Our Pond

The pond in our garden
Is murky and deep
And lots of things live there
That slither and creep,

Like diving bell spiders
And great ramshorn snails
And whirligig beetles
And black snappertails.

There used to be goldfish
That nibbled my thumb,
But now there's just algae
And sour, crusty scum.

There used to be pondweed
With fizzy green shoots,
But now there are leeches
And horrible newts.

One day when my football
Rolled in by mistake
I tried to retrieve it
By using a rake,

But as I leaned over
A shape from the ooze
Bulged up like a nightmare
And lunged at my shoes.

I ran back in shouting,
But everyone laughed
And said I was teasing
Or else I was daft.

But I know what happened
And when I'm asleep
I dream of those creatures
That slither and creep:

The diving bell spiders
And great ramshorn snails
And whirligig beetles
And black snappertails.

Richard Edwards

29

Water Striders

Ittery, skittery,
Water bugs prance.
On top of the water
They dawdle and dance,

Drifting together,
Then scrambling apart —
Ittery, skittery,
Dimple and dart!

Edith E. Cutting

Gray Squirrel

Hurry, hurry, scamper, scurry,
Little squirrel all gray and furry.
Find an acorn; crack it, crunch it,
Nibble, nibble, munch, munch, munch it.
Find another, fat and round,
To bury quickly in the ground.
Gather nuts — don't stop to play!
For winter winds are on the way.

Joan Horton

A Swallow and Me

It must be fun being a swallow,
Flying straight as an arrow,
Darting sharp corners
In the air,
Sailing swift on the winds,
Catching bugs in the sky,
Wearing bright colored feathers
For cover
In all weathers,
And never needing a coat or hat.
I wish I could be like that.

But when a swallow looks down
And sees me on the ground
The swallow might think
"Being a kid must be fun.
Kids can jump. Kids can run.
Kids can throw and catch a ball,

And that's not all.
Kids can do lots of tricks
And can make pretty pictures
With those bright
Colored sticks.
Kids can wear a coat and hat.
I wish I could be like that."

But I guess the best thing
Is for a swallow bird to be
How a swallow bird should be
And for a kid to be
How a kid should be
And for me to be
Just me.

Rhoda Gersten

The Snake

A narrow fellow in the grass
Occasionally rides;
You may have met him, — did you not,
His notice sudden is.

The grass divides as with a comb,
A spotted shaft is seen;
And then it closes at your feet
And opens further on.

He likes a boggy acre,
A floor too cool for corn.
Yet when a child, and barefoot,
I more than once, at morn,

34

Have passed, I thought, a whip-lash
Unbraiding in the sun, —
When, stooping to secure it,
It wrinkled, and was gone.

Several of nature's people
I know, and they know me;
I feel for them a transport
Of cordiality;

But never met this fellow,
Attended or alone,
Without a tighter breathing,
And zero to the bone.

Emily Dickinson

35

Baboon

Hairy baby,
lightly bounding,
brightly, briskly
through the trees,
somersaults and
lies down backwards,
stays there balanced
in the leaves,
grabs a branch and swings out easy
swings out free —
baboon trapeze!

Ann Whitford Paul

The Tiger

In the immensity of the jungle
the orange tiger lives.
Silently he moves
and gives
the soft sound of his padded feet
back to the silent night.
The hot wind blows,
the treetops bend
and sway beneath the cloud gray sky.
And where the water spills
cold from the distant hills,
he crouches low to drink.

Joan E. Cass

37

Gray Owl

When fireflies begin to wink
over the stubble near the wood,
ghost-of-the-air,
the gray owl, glides into dusk

Over the spruce, a drift of smoke,
over the juniper knoll,
whispering wings
making the sound of silk unfurling,
in the soft blur of starlight
a puff of feathers blown about.

Terrible fixed eyes,
talons sheathed in down,
refute this floating wraith.

Before the shapes of mist
show white beneath the moon,
the rabbit or the rat
will know the knives of fire,
the pothooks swinging out of space.

But now the muffled hunter
moves like smoke, like wind,
scarcely apprehended,
barely glimpsed and gone,
like a gray thought
fanning the margins of the mind.

Joseph Payne Brennan

Acknowledgments

Poems with attributed authors are listed in order of appearance; all other entries are anonymous:

"Beasts and Birds" by Adelaide O'Keeffe; "Warm Paws" by Brian Patten; "The Shark" by Lord Alfred Douglas, reproduced by kind permission of Mrs. Sheila Colman; "Ducks' Ditty from *The Wind in the Willows* by Kenneth Grahame, copyright © The University Chest, Oxford, reproduced by permission of Curtis Brown Ltd, London; "An Introduction to Dogs" by Ogden Nash, from *Verses from 1929* by Ogden Nash, copyright © 1936 by Ogden Nash, reproduced by kind permission of Little, Brown and Company; "First Came L. E. Phant's Letter" by Countee Cullen; "Lion" by Barbara Juster Esbensen; "Nicholas Nye" (extract) by Walter de la Mare, from *The Complete Poems of Walter de la Mare*, reproduced by kind permission of the Literary Trustees of Walter de la Mare, and the Society of Authors as their representative; "The Corn Scratch Kwa Kwa Hen and the Fox" by Julie Holder; "Hyena," Anon., translated by Ulli Beier; "The Spider" by Frank Collymore; "The Kitten Playing with the Falling Leaves" by William Wordsworth; "Our Pond" by Richard Edwards, from *The Word Party*, reproduced by kind permission of James Clarke & Co. Ltd, The Lutterworth Press; "Water Striders" by Edith E. Cutting, reprinted by kind permission of *Ladybug* magazine, June 1997, Vol. 7, No.10, copyright © 1997 by Edith E. Cutting; "Gray Squirrel" by Joan Horton, reproduced by kind permission of Joan Horton; "A Swallow and Me" by Rhoda Gersten, reprinted by kind permission of *Spider* magazine, September 1996, Vol. 3, No. 9, copyright © 1996 by Rhoda Gersten; "The Snake" by Emily Dickinson; "Baboon" by Ann Whitford Paul, reproduced by kind permission of Ann Whitford Paul; "The Tiger" by Joan E. Cass; "Gray Owl" by Joseph Payne Brennan.

The publishers have made every effort to contact holders of copyright material. If you have not received our correspondence, please contact us for inclusion in future editions.

BAREFOOT BOOKS publishes high-quality picture books for
children of all ages and specializes in the work of artists and writers from
many cultures. If you have enjoyed this book and would like to receive a copy of
our current catalog, please contact our New York office —
Barefoot Books Inc., 37 West 17th Street, 4th Floor East, New York, New York, 10010
e-mail: ussales@barefoot-books.com   website: www.barefoot-books.com